the Son of the Sun and the Daughter of the Moon

8-00

To my husband, Tom, whose work has
taken us to exotic places and inspired
my writing. Thank you for your
constant support.

–H.H.

For Mathis

–A.V.

Atheneum Books for Young Readers
An imprint of Simon & Schuster Children's Publishing Division
1230 Avenue of the Americas
New York, New York 10020
Text copyright © 2000 by Holly Young Huth
Illustration copyright © 2000 by Anna Vojtech
All rights reserved, including the right of reproduction in whole or in part in any form.
Book design by Angela Carlino
The text of this book is set in Mrs. Eaves.
The illustrations are rendered in watercolor.
Printed in Hong Kong
10 9 8 7 6 5 4 3 2 1
Library of Congress Cataloging-in-Publication Data
Huth, Holly Young.
The son of the sun and the daughter of the moon: a Saami folktale / retold by Holly Young
Huth; illustrated by Anna Vojtech.
p. cm.
Summary: Solvake, the son of the sun, wants to marry the daughter of the moon, but she has
other plans.
ISBN 0-689-82482-3
1. Sami (European people)—Folklore. [1. Sun—Folklore. 2. Moon—Folklore. 3. Sami
(European people)—Folklore. 4. Folklore—Russia.] I. Vojtech, Anna, ill. II. Title.
PZ8.1.H98So 1999 398.2'089'9455—dc21 98-44731

FIRST
EDITION

A SAAMI FOLKTALE
AS TOLD BY HOLLY YOUNG HUTH

the Son of the Sun and the Daughter of the Moon

ILLUSTRATED BY ANNA VOJTECH

ATHENEUM BOOKS FOR YOUNG READERS

Through all the hours of the long, long day, the sun labors in the sky, making warm light to keep the earth alive. He throws down sunbeam upon sunbeam while the reindeer and the bear take turns pulling him across the heavens in a sled.

In the evenings he wants nothing more than to sleep. But one night he was pestered by his son, Solvake.

"I must find a wife," Solvake said. "I have tried my golden boots on many Earth maidens, but none yet has been able to fly away with me."

"I will ask the moon for you," his father said. "I have heard she has a new daughter."

So one morning, when the moon lingered in the sky, the sun approached her: "I hear that you have a lovely daughter. My son would like to be her suitor."

Mother Moon's bright face darkened. "My daughter is too young to marry," she said.

"We at the House of the Sun will care for her until she is of age to marry," the sun insisted.

"No," the moon said, and quickly covered her daughter with a cloud.

The sun became furious. He hurled fiery arrows. Thunder shook the skies. Wind knocked over trees and houses, and the sea turned upside down. "Have you forgotten my great strength? I give life to all things. I will marry my son to your daughter!" he roared.

"The son of a hot-headed sun is no match for my daughter," said the moon. Holding her daughter close, she hurried off.

Mother Moon searched the northern lands for a safe place to hide her daughter from the eyes of the sun.

At last she found a kind old woman and a kind old man living
alone on an island in the middle of a lake.

When the sun's fury was finally spent and the earth settled down, the old woman and the old man walked through the woods to see the storm's damage. There they saw a silver cradle hanging from a branch.

When they first looked in, they found the cradle empty. But then they heard a child's voice: "Now I vanish. Now I return."

When they looked in the cradle a second time, they saw a child. She looked like an ordinary child except that she gleamed with moonlight. They gave her the name "Vanishia," for the vanishing game she played.

The old couple were pleased to finally have a daughter of their own. They treated her well and taught her how to make clothes and blankets out of reindeer skin and to embroider with colorful beads.

Vanishia grew up to be a lovely young woman with skin that was fresh and rosy like cloudberries. It was not long before rumors reached the sun of a mysterious woman whose ways were more skybound than those of most women on Earth. So the sun sent Solvake to find this fabled woman.

Flying over the island, Solvake spied Vanishia and fell out of the sky, instantly in love. Landing at her feet, he said, "I am the son of the sun and my golden boots are yours. Try them, please."

Vanishia blushed as she tried them on. "But they burn my feet!" she protested.

"You'll get used to them soon," Solvake promised.

But Vanishia simply said, "Now I am gone!" And she vanished, leaving nothing but the empty boots where she had stood.

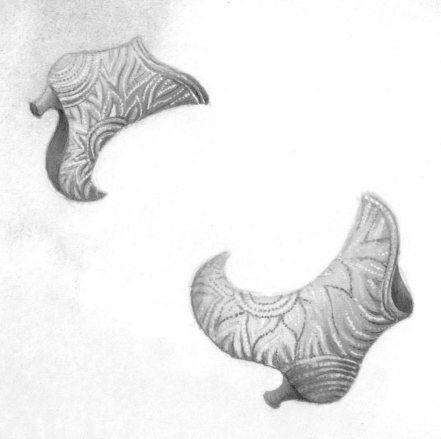

Seeing her daughter's distress, Mother Moon led her across the lake, over the tundra to a desolate cabin by the sea.

Inside, the cabin was so drab and untidy, Vanishia decided to scrub it clean and fill it with flowers. Then, exhausted, she saw a blanket chest, crawled inside, and fell fast asleep.

At twilight she was awakened by heavy footsteps. Vanishia peered from beneath the lid of the chest. Warriors in silver armor entered the house. They were the Brothers of the Northern Lights, handsome and strong.

"A woman's hands have graced our home. I feel her eyes watching us. Where could she be?" said Luminias, their leader. During the warriors' meal, Luminias puzzled in silence.

Afterward, the brothers' swords and shields clattered as they battled in play until they tired and fell asleep. When they woke, they sang of warriors in the sky and then flew off, one after the other—all but Luminias.

Left alone, Luminias spoke to the empty room. "I know that you are here," he said. "And although we have not met, I feel a bond between us. Please come forth."

"Now I am here," Vanishia said, appearing suddenly before him. As soon as their eyes met, love moved into their hearts. And that night, before Luminias rejoined his brothers in the sky, they were married under the light of Mother Moon.

Every morning Luminias and the Brothers of the Northern Lights came home to dine. They played their battle game, slept, and then flew away again at sunset. They were careful to travel through darkening skies to avoid the sun.

"Please, can't you stay with me for just one full day and night," Vanishia begged Luminias.

"No, my love, I must always return over the sea to the battle of the skies."
But one afternoon while Luminias slept, Vanishia tricked him into
staying longer by hanging over the windows a bright cloth with an
embroidered sun. When he awoke that night, he thought that it was only
midday and whiled away the hours with his wife.

When he finally opened the door, he was shocked to see the sun was about to rise. He ran outside to search for his brothers. It was then that the sun saw him, and with a flaming arrow pinned him to the ground.

Vanishia rushed over to pull the fiery arrow from Luminias's body, but it was too late. All that was left of him was a pale shadow that rose into the sky over the sea.

The sun grabbed Vanishia by her long hair. His fiery presence
burned her skin as he called for his son.

"I will never marry Solvake," Vanishia wept. "You'll have to kill
me first."

Furious, the sun flung Vanishia away from him, high into the
sky.

There, Mother Moon caught her daughter and held her close to her heart. To this day, Vanishia rests in her mother's arms. If you look carefully, you can see the shadow of her face on the moon.

She is always watching. She is watching the pale shadow over the
sea. She is watching the battle of the Northern Lights in the sky.
Nothing can tear her eyes away from it.